To
Carli,
Norman is
nuts about you!!.
= Laura
April 19, 2013

THiS BOOk BeLONGS tO:

Dear Parents, Caregivers and Teachers,

Help your child find the hidden peanuts. Since looking for peanuts is what leads Norman along through the book, the illustrator has carefully hidden a peanut somewhere within each illustration. Ask your child to join Norman in the hunt for peanuts. The answers to the hidden peanuts are found on page 48.

The Story of Norman is a cautionary tale about rules, disobedience, and consequences. Norman, not unlike us humans, becomes focused on what he is not supposed to have then casually begins inching his way towards it. When he manages to escape getting caught the first time, confidence in his ability flairs into blatant disobedience. Finally, when his own might fails, his father's words and his friend's pleadings become real.

As our children grow and are faced with unwise choices, opportunities to break family rules, or maybe begin considering harmful things, it is my hope they will remember Norman's plight, pause, and think ahead to the outcome.

The Story of Norman in the Forest continues with experiences that help to develop solid character in the young squirrel as he works his way back home.

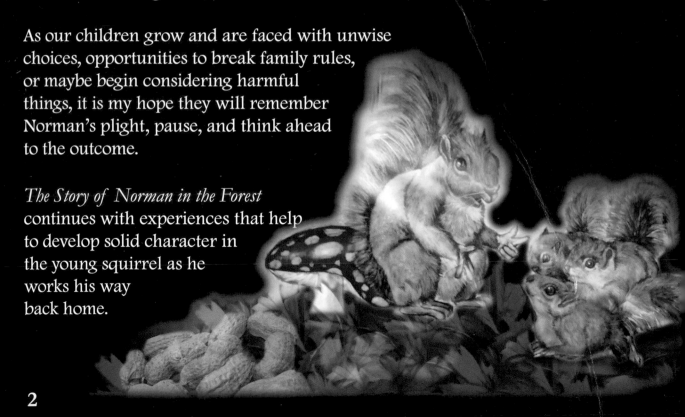

the story of

Norman

By Laura JK Chamberlain
Illustrated by Donna Brooks

Heart to Heart   Publishing, Inc.

Heart to Heart Publishing, Inc,
528 Mud Creek Road • Morgantown, KY 42261
(270) 526-5589
www.hearttoheartpublishinginc.com

Printed in U.S.A.
Walsworth
306 N. Kansas Ave
Marceline, MO 64658

Copyright 2010 Laura JK Chamberlain
Publishing Date January 2011
Library of Congress : 2010942799
ISBN 9780-9802486-9

Senior Editor: L.J. Gill
Editor: Jan Black Embry
Copy-Editor & Proofreader: Evelyn Byers
Illustrator: Donna Brooks
Designer: April Yingling

Author
Dedicated to my husband, Kevin Dawson, squirrel
evictor extraordinaire and to our wonderful
grandchildren, Emily, Taylor, Ryann,
Addison, and Mason
~ Laura JK Chamberlain

Illustrator
I'd like to give special thanks to a wonderful
loving God who has blessed me in so many ways,
especially giving me two precious grandchildren,
Abby & Ethan.   These two keep me young
at heart, body, soul, & mind.
~ Donna Brooks

Springtime had finally arrived in the forest where Norman lived. The last patches of snow had melted away, and warm sunshine made the forest animals peek out of their winter homes. Sweet grasses and fresh flowers were sprouting all across the land. It had been a long winter, so all the forest animals were eager to begin running and playing again: that is, all of them except Norman.

Norman was a young squirrel who lived with his parents in a cozy nest in the tippy top of the tallest tree in the whole forest. While all the forest animals were shouting, running, and rolling around in the new spring grass, Norman wasn't interested. He was only thinking about one thing: food!

"I have been eating the same old seeds and pine cones all winter long! I want something different. I want peanuts!" exclaimed Norman.

"Norman," said Mother, "Why don't you go out and play with your friends? Everyone is having such a good time now that spring is finally here."

"I'm hungry. I want some peanuts," whined Norman.

"There are no peanuts in the forest," scolded Mother. "Only people living in the village over the hill have peanuts and you know what your father says about that."

"I know," sassed Norman, "'*It is much too dangerous to go over there, Son. A young squirrel could get into a lot of trouble going near people.*' That's what he always says!"

"Now, Norman," said Mother, "Your father and I know what is best for you and we do not want you to go near people. It is just not safe! Why don't you scamper over to the glen and gather some fresh toadstools before they are all gone? I will fix your favorite meal: Toadstool Delight with tender tree buds sprinkled on top. Would you like that?"

"I suppose," moped Norman and he scurried down the tree.

8

"Hi ya, Norm!" called Cedrick, Norman's best friend. "Whatcha doin'?"

"I'm going to the dumb old glen to collect toadstools for my mother," Norman moaned.

"Hey, can I go with ya, Norm? Huh? Can I? Can I go, too?" begged Cedrick.

"I suppose," said Norman and the two friends darted off toward the glen.

But they never got there!

As they neared the edge of the forest, Norman heard something strange. "What's that noise?" he asked.

"Um, I don't hear anything," said Cedrick, looking all around.

"It's coming from over that hill. Let's go see," urged Norman, running up the hillside.

"Whoa! Would you look at that!" he said, gazing at a brand new neighborhood that had just been built right at the edge of the forest.

"Yikes!" shrieked Cedrick. "People! We'd better get outta here!"

"Peanuts!" shouted Norman.

"Huh?" asked Cedrick, looking over at his friend rather confused.

"Peanuts! Where there are people, there must be peanuts and I have been thinking about eating peanuts all winter long! Let's take a closer look."

"No way!" said Cedrick, trying to stop his friend. "You know the rules. Now, come on, let's get goin' to the glen before all the good toadstools are gone."

"I just want to take a closer look. Don't worry so much. Nothing is going to happen," said Norman, scampering toward the biggest house on the entire block.

"Norman, no! It is too dangerous!" called Cedrick. But it was too late. Norman had already gone. Cedrick did not know what to do so he called out, "Wait for me, Norman!" and ran after him.

13

Norman had never seen anything so exciting in all his life-big buildings, pointed roof tops, long rain gutters, and fancy porch trusses! "What perfect places to sit and watch all the people go by while eating fresh, crunchy peanuts," he said, jumping up and down.

Cedrick was too scared to be excited. He just wanted to go back to the forest where it was safe.

Norman began sniffing the air, "Peanuts! I smell peanuts, and it is coming from over there!"...off he rushed to a nearby deck. "They are in there," he whispered to Cedrick as they looked at the strange pack lying on a bench.

Using his sharp teeth, Norman began to chew a hole in the canvas pack until finally he had it! A bag of peanuts! Just as he pulled it out through the hole, the patio door flew open! Cedrick's eyes grew big as saucers when he saw a huge broom sweeping toward him. He jumped straight up in the air, then took off running. First, this way, then that way he ran until finally he was safely back at the edge of the forest. Huffing and puffing, he looked around for Norman.

"Norm?" he whispered. "Pssst, Norm. Where are ya, buddy?"

There was no answer.

14

Looking up, Cedrick was amazed at what he saw next. There, on the top of the roof of the tallest house in the entire neighborhood sat Norman, still holding the bag of peanuts. "Come on down!" signaled Cedrick. "Get down from there and let's go!"

Norman shook his head *"no"* and held up one finger telling his friend to wait just a minute. Then he began to explore his new surroundings. Cedrick watched from the forest hill as Norman found a tiny opening at the roof's edge. First his head, then his legs, then finally his long bushy tail disappeared into the hole. Cedrick's very best friend, Norman, was gone.

"Honey, I have been hearing a strange noise in the house," said Mrs. Butterman to her husband, Joe Butterman. "I think it is coming from the roof."

"I'll check it out," he said, going to get his ladder. "It might be squirrels running across the rooftop."

Joe Butterman climbed his ladder to the top of his very tall house and looked all around trying to discover what was making the strange noise.

"Hmm," said Joe Butterman to himself. "There is a tiny round hole here at the roof's edge. I wonder how that got there. Well, I'd better patch it right away before any squirrels get in there." And down the ladder he went.

Soon Joe Butterman returned wearing leather gloves and carrying a hammer, some nails, a set of pliers and a piece of screen-wire. He set to work repairing the hole in the roof's edge. As he worked, shaping and cutting the screen that would soon fit perfectly over the hole, he began to wonder, *"If a squirrel is in this hole right now and I patch it shut, he won't be able to get out. I'd better check in there first."* So, Joe Butterman stuck his hand inside the hole and felt all around to make sure there was no squirrel in there.

20

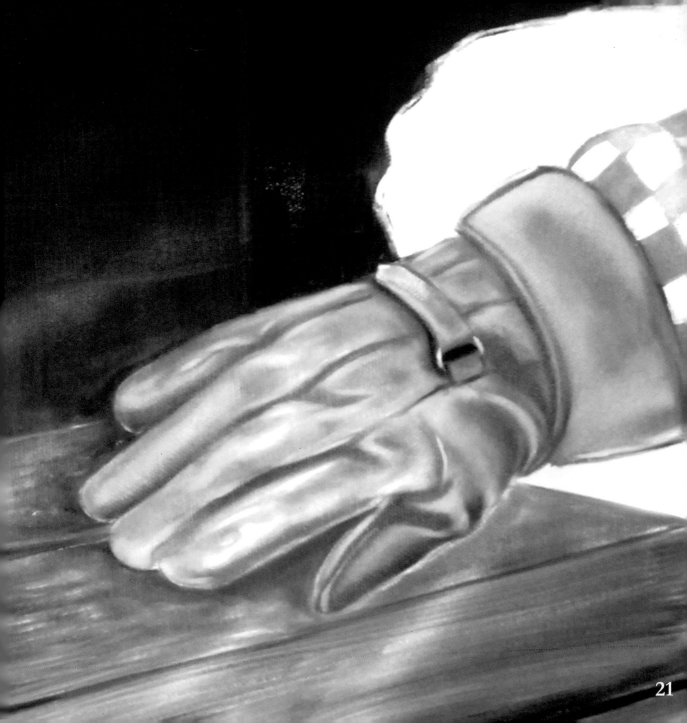

Meanwhile, Norman had found a cozy bunch of leaves to sit on while he looked at all the peanuts he had gathered. He had lined them up in a row so he could see them and count them and smell them. He was very happy.

Suddenly, a big leather hand appeared right in front of him. It reached and felt and scooped all around the new area Norman had just fixed. Frightened, Norman quickly pressed himself flat against the wall.

SWISH went the leather hand, just missing Norman. *SWISH* it came back around again, this time almost touching Norman's floppy tail. He tucked his tail tightly behind him, pressed his back up against the wall and sucked in his fat tummy. He stood frozen as the leather hand patted all around just missing him several times. Then it was gone. Norman breathed a sigh of relief and finally let his long bushy tail go free.

"Whew, that was close!" he said. He began to laugh, "Cedrick is so afraid of people. Ha! And my father warns, *'A young squirrel could get into a lot of trouble going near people.'* Ha, ha, ha. A squirrel just has to be smart like me and never get caught!"

Norman felt very proud of himself.

Joe Butterman was putting his ladder away while telling Mrs. Butterman all about patching the hole at the roof's edge. "No squirrels can get in there now. I fixed it nice and tight." They went inside to eat their supper.

It was getting late. Norman decided he'd better hurry and eat his peanuts. He needed to get back to the forest before anyone found out he had broken the rules and went into the village. When the last wonderful, round, delicious peanut was gone, Norman dove, head first, into the very same round hole he had used to get into his new hiding place. "BOING!" His head hit something and he bounced right back. *That's strange*, he thought. Again he pushed through the hole at the roof's edge, and "BOING!" Again he bounced right back. *What is this?* Norman looked more closely at the screen and realized he was trapped with no way out and no more food!

"Cedrick!" yelled Norman. "Cedrick, go get my father! Cedrick, I'm trapped up here! Go get help for me!" But Cedrick did not hear. Norman was really and truly stuck.

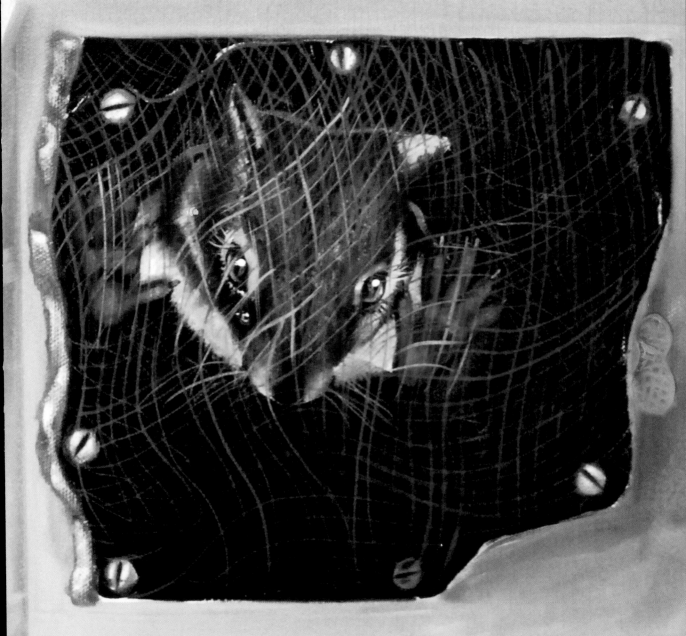

27

All night long Norman sat looking out the wire patch Joe Butterman had nailed over the hole. He bit it, shook it, and pushed it. Still, it would not move. Norman began to cry.

The next day, after Joe Butterman left for work, Norman decided to look for another way out. "I'll have to chew my way out!" he told himself, trying to be brave. Using his very sharp teeth he began to bite, gnaw, claw, and chew his way through the wall under the roof's edge. Even though he was very hungry and very tired, he kept chewing and gnawing. Finally he had made a hole big enough to fit through.

"Whoa!" said Norman as he dropped down into the strange new place he had discovered. "It's huge in here! I wonder if there are any peanuts?" And he began to explore.

29

When Joe Butterman arrived home from work that evening, Mrs. Butterman told him, "Dear, I have been hearing a strange noise in the house, I think this time it is coming from the attic."

"I'll check it out," said Joe Butterman, opening the attic door. "I hope squirrels did not get in there."

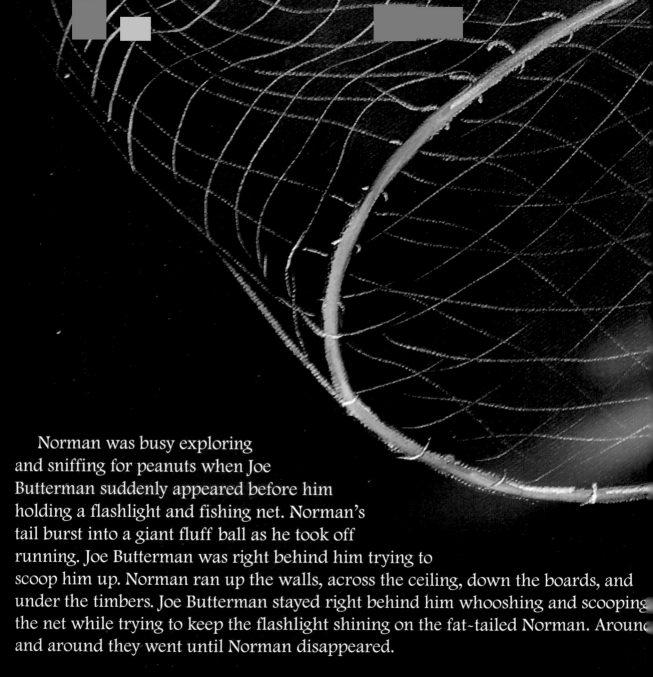

Norman was busy exploring
and sniffing for peanuts when Joe
Butterman suddenly appeared before him
holding a flashlight and fishing net. Norman's
tail burst into a giant fluff ball as he took off
running. Joe Butterman was right behind him trying to
scoop him up. Norman ran up the walls, across the ceiling, down the boards, and
under the timbers. Joe Butterman stayed right behind him whooshing and scooping
the net while trying to keep the flashlight shining on the fat-tailed Norman. Around
and around they went until Norman disappeared.

Joe Butterman finally gave up, went back downstairs, and told Mrs. Butterman all about his adventure of trying to capture Norman. Then he got an idea, "I'll go into town tomorrow and get a trap for the little guy. We'll catch him."

After awhile, Norman poked his head out from his hiding place and realized Joe Butterman was gone. "Whew, that was close!" he sighed. Then he began to laugh, "Cedrick is so afraid of people. Ha! And my father warns, *'A young squirrel could get in a lot of trouble going near people.'* Ha, ha, ha. A squirrel just has to be smart like me and never get caught!" He was very proud of himself.

The next day, Joe Butterman placed a trap in the attic.

"It won't hurt him will it, dear?" asked Mrs. Butterman.

"Of course it won't," he explained. "We just have to get him to walk in here, causing this door to slam shut. Then he won't be able to get out. After that, we will take him to the edge of the forest and let him go. He won't bother us any more, but we need to find something to make him go into the trap."

"How about these?" asked Mrs. Butterman, holding out a handful of peanuts.

"Ah, yes, the perfect thing," agreed Joe Butterman, and very carefully he set the trap.

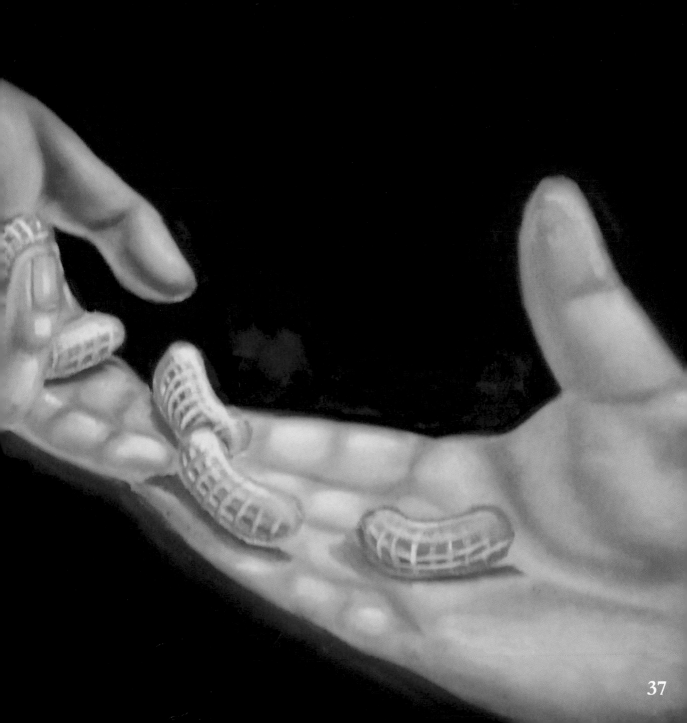

Norman had been stuck in the attic for a long time now and he was getting pretty hungry. "I wish I could find something good to eat. I am so hungry I would even eat a big fat toadstool with Cedrick. I really miss my friend," he said, feeling a tear come to his eye.

At first, Norman thought he was dreaming because he kept smelling peanuts. *Mmmmm, wonderful, round, delicious peanuts,* he thought. All at once, he realized it was not a dream at all. He really was smelling peanuts, but where?

Norman began to look around. Soon, he found a strange looking box. *That's odd*, he thought while poking the box with his paw. That is when he saw them! Right there, just inside the strange box was his heart's desire. The most wonderful thing in Norman's world; PEANUTS! He did not even stop to think for one second. He just jumped right inside the trap and grabbed a paw full of peanuts. Before he could shove them into his mouth, he heard a dreadful sound:

SLAM!

The door to the cage had slammed shut and Norman was trapped inside. *OH NO!* He thought. There was no way out. He clawed and he chewed, he dug and he bit, but he could not free himself from Joe Butterman's trap.

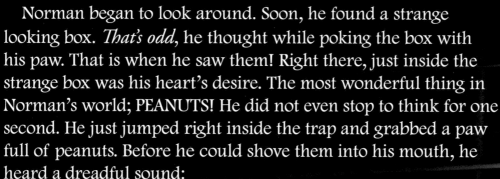

As the cage holding Norman bounced around in the back end of Joe Butterman's rusty old pick-up truck, the little squirrel was not feeling very proud. He remembered his father's warning, *"A young squirrel could get into a lot of trouble going near people."* He thought about Cedrick telling him to stop. He wished he had obeyed the rules. He wanted to be safe at home in the forest, rolling around in the new spring grass with his friends and eating Toadstool Delight with his family. Instead, he was trapped in a cage. Norman was so ashamed.

After driving many miles down a winding, dusty road, Joe Butterman stopped the truck and got out. He held the cage up, smiled at Norman and said, "Hello, little guy. You'd better hurry on home, now. Your family is probably worried about you." Then he walked to the edge of the forest, opened the cage door and shook Norman out.

Once Norman realized he was free, his tail burst into a giant fluff ball and he took off running. Joe Butterman laughed, got back into his truck and drove away. Norman ran and ran and ran. He did not stop running until he was safe, deep inside the forest.

Many years passed. Cedrick was with his family in their cozy nest in the tippy top of a very tall tree. "Daddy, tell us about the time Norman disobeyed his parents and ended up alone in the forest," asked his young son.

"I've already told you that story," said Cedrick in his deep fatherly voice.

"We want to hear it again, Daddy!" begged his daughters. "Please tell us the story of Norman."

"Okay," said Cedrick, and his children scurried over to listen. Thinking about that day, he began…

"Springtime had finally arrived in the forest where Norman lived. The last patches of snow had melted away and warm sunshine made the forest animals peel out of their winter homes. Sweet grasses and fresh flowers were sprouting all across the land. It had been a long winter so all the forest animals were eager to begin running and playing again: that is, all of them except Norman."

Peanut  Search